THE BOY AND THE DOVE

THE BOY AND THE DOVE

Story by James Sage

Photographs by Robert Doisneau

with the artistic collaboration of Pierre Derlon

WORKMAN PUBLISHING COMPANY / NEW YORK

Editorial direction and design by Aileen Friedman

The authors wish to express their appreciation to Raymond and Barbara Grosset of Rapho Agence de Presse, Paris.

Library of Congress Cataloging in Publication Data

Doisneau, Robert. The boy and the dove.
    SUMMARY: When school begins in the fall, a
young boy and his dove, once inseparable, find a
new way to be together.
    [1. Pigeons—Fiction]   I. Sage, James
II. Title
PZ7.D697Bo   [E]   77-18427
ISBN 0-89480-030-2
ISBN 0-89480-072-2 pbk.

Workman Publishing Company
1 West 39th Street
New York, New York 10018

Manufactured in the United States of America
First printing May 1978

10 9 8 7 6 5 4 3 2 1

A mon ami Pierre Derlon, lanceur de graines et charmeur d'oiseaux,
A sa terre la Princesse Claude, qui refuse de lire dans les mains et se
    contente d'être sa ligne de chance.   —ROBERT DOISNEAU

For Alexandra   —JAMES SAGE

Once there was a boy who dreamed of having a dove of his own. This dove would be his special friend.

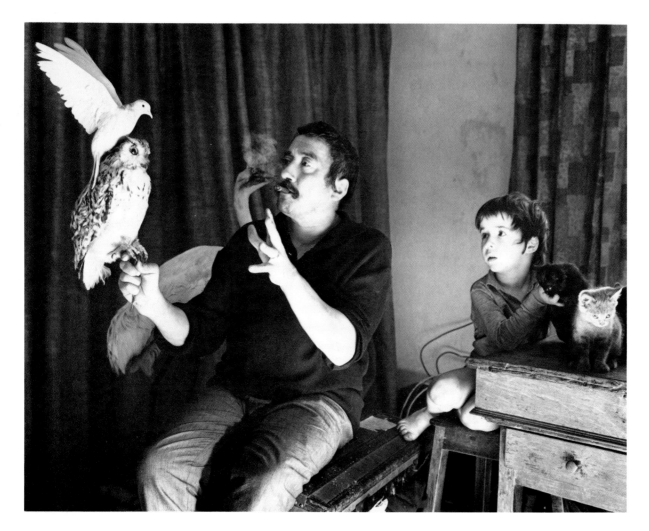

The boy's father trained birds for the theatre, so there were always many doves in his house. But not one of the doves belonged to the boy.

One day his father said: "It is time you had a dove that is yours alone. He will be your dream come true."

The next day they went to the bird market.
"Oh, what a beautiful dove!" said the boy.

"Now he is yours," said his father. "He is yours
to love and care for."

The boy thought: Someday I may train him. But first we will just become friends.

At home, the boy worried that others in his family
might not like his new friend.

But his mother said: "Do not worry, little one.
We will learn to live in peace."

Even the cats tried to make the dove feel at home...
all except Bibi, who pretended not to care.

Soon the dove felt very much at home, and the boy imagined they would never be apart.

The two of them went everywhere.

The dove was particularly pleased when the boy took him shopping
in the market...

for reasons best known to doves.

When his errands were done, the boy treated his friend to a cool glass of water...

and the dove would drink slowly, with small sips, as doves do.

Then they had to hurry home.

For the hour would be late and everyone would be waiting.

All summer long, the boy and the dove played together.

Finally, the day came when the boy had to return to school.

"Do not worry," he told the dove. "You will not be lonely.
I will take you with me."

On the way to school, he stopped to show the dove to his friend on the bridge.

"What a fine bird!" the old man said. "And I notice he does not fly away. He must love you very much."

"Yes," said the boy. "We are always together. I am even taking him to school with me. But one day, I will do as my father does and train him to perform in the theatre."

When his classmates saw the dove, the boy began
to wonder if he had not made a mistake.

Everyone teased the bird and shouted and whistled at him. The boy felt very sad about the way they treated his friend.

Suddenly, the dove flew around and around the room.

The commotion made everyone laugh
except the boy.

It was impossible for him to pay attention.

The teacher was very angry.

"This is not a zoo!" she scolded. "We must leave our pets at home."

The boy tried to remember his lessons, but all he could think about was what the teacher had said. How could he leave his dove at home?

He told his story to the old man on the bridge.

"I do not want my dove to be lonely," said the boy.

"He would not be lonely at the theatre," answered the man. "Did you not tell me that someday you would train your dove? Perhaps the time has come. You can ask your father to help you."

When the boy showed how skillful his dove could be, his father said: "There is no doubt that he is a born performer. We can certainly train him."

But then he added: "If your dove becomes a performer, he may have to live at the theatre. I am sure the two of you will stay the best of friends, but you may not see each other often. Are you certain that you want to train him?"

The boy tried to decide what would be best for his dove. Finally, he answered his father. "Yes," the boy said.

And so the training began.

The boy was proud that the dove learned quickly. He looked forward to the day when his bird would perform for everyone. But the boy hoped that he and his friend would not be apart for long.

Soon it was time to take the dove to the theatre.

The boy's dove was much admired by the dancers in the ballet,
who said they had never seen such a clever bird.

When the leading dancer saw him, she exclaimed: "I must have him for my ballet! He will become a star."

Then she said: "Your dove must live at the theatre. Will you come here after school and train him for me?"

The boy agreed and was happy, for he and his friend would still be together.

Everyday, when his lessons were done, the boy trained the dove at the theatre.

Sometimes they rehearsed on the great stage.

The training was very hard work, but the boy did not mind. The dove was happy and so was he.

On weekends, the boy stayed backstage while his dove performed.

Between acts, they sat together.

When the ballet company was on vacation,
the dove would go home with the boy.

As time passed, the story of the boy and the dove became well-known. Wherever they went, people would ask:

"Aren't you the boy with the clever friend?"

"Aren't you the boy with the dream come true?"

ROBERT DOISNEAU is a Frenchman and a humanist. He is also that rarity, a humorist with the camera.

Doisneau first took up free-lance photography in 1939, at the age of twenty-seven, after five years as an industrial photographer. It was not until after the war that he was able to indulge his passion for recording the life he found on endless promenades along the streets of his beloved Paris.

Over the years, these images formed the basis for numerous books, exhibitions, and articles and brought his work to the attention of an international audience. "The Boy and the Dove" is the outgrowth of a friendship with the family that is portrayed in the book. The situations were photographed in Paris, as they occurred.

JAMES SAGE has long been associated with photography, first through filmmaking and later as a picture editor and photographers' agent. While working in the latter capacity, he discovered the photographs that illustrate "The Boy and the Dove."

Mr. Sage and his wife and daughter now reside in Scotland. His many activities include writing about photography and photographers.

PIERRE DERLON has devoted a number of years to studying and writing about the life of Gypsies. By adopting their attitude that all work is normal and welcome, he has at various times been employed as stuntman, clown, house painter, private detective, art teacher, stagehand, and bird trainer.

It was while he was working as a bird trainer for the ballet of the Marquis de Cuevas that the photographs in this book were taken.

AILEEN FRIEDMAN is a native of Baltimore. She has worked in New York since the 1960's as an editor, book designer, art director, and publishing consultant. She is also a writer and is the author of "The Castles of the Two Brothers."